S0-BYA-086
04/2014

PALM BEACH COUNTY
LIBRARY SYSTEM
3650 Summit Boulevard
West Palm Beach. FL 33406-4198

THE DENTIST FROM THE BLACK LAGOON

STORY BY
MIKE THALER

PICTURES BY
JARED LEE

Cartwheel
B·O·O·K·S ®

SCHOLASTIC INC.

New York   Toronto   London   Auckland   Sydney
Mexico City   New Delhi   Hong Kong   Buenos Aires

To Dr. Solberg and Joanne, only kidding!—M.T.
To all the friendly dentists everywhere who take good care of our teeth.—J.L.

visit us at www.abdopublishing.com

Reinforced library bound edition published in 2014 by Spotlight, a division of the ABDO Group, PO Box 398166, Minneapolis, MN 55439. Spotlight produces high-quality reinforced library bound editions for schools and libraries. Published by agreement with Scholastic, Inc.

Printed in the United States of America, North Mankato, Minnesota.
102013
012014
This book contains at least 10% recycled materials.

Text copyright © 2005 by Mike Thaler. Illustrations copyright © 2005 by Jared D. Lee Studio, Inc. All rights reserved. Published by Scholastic, Inc. No part of this book may be reproduced, stored in a retrieval system, or tranmitted in any form or by any means, electronic, mechanical, photocopying, recording, or otherwise, without written permission of the publisher. For information regarding permission, write to Scholastic, Inc., Attention: Permissions Department
557 Broadway, New York, New York 10012.

Cataloging-in-Publication Data

Thaler, Mike, 1936-
  The dentist from the black lagoon / by Mike Thaler ; pictures by Jared Lee.
  p. cm. -- (Black Lagoon)
  Summary: A boy learns that a dentist will be visiting his school. He hears scary rumors about the dentist, but discovers there is no reason to be afraid of dentists.
  1. Dentists--Fiction. 2. Fear--Fiction. I. Title. II Series.
  PZ7.T3 De 2005
  [Fic]--dc23

ISBN 978-1-61479-197-3 (Reinforced Library Bound Edition)

All Spotlight books are reinforced library binding
and manufactured in the United States of America.

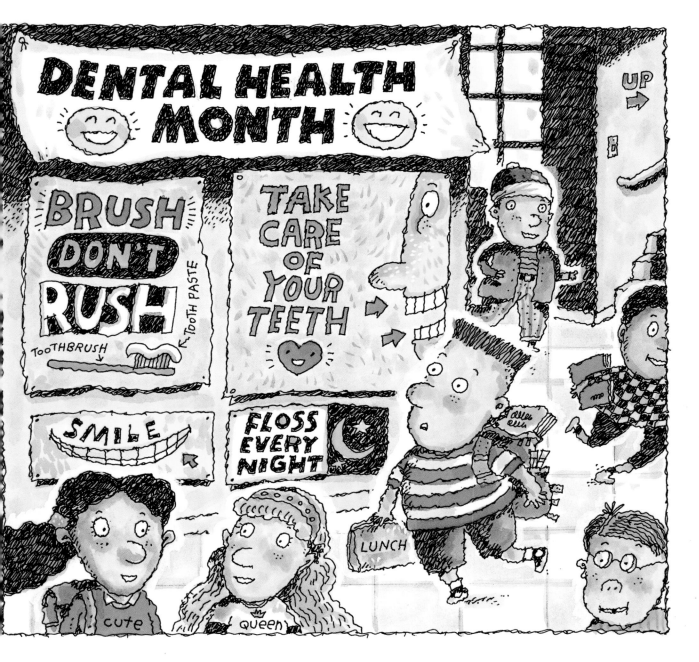

Uh-oh, it's Dental Health month!

SUN

TOOTH FAIRY

Miss Hearse, the nurse, says there's a real dentist coming on Friday. His name is Dr. B.N. Payne.

He's bringing his equipment, and he's going to check our teeth.

YELLOW BUG

AUNT

I don't want checked teeth…

maybe polka-dotted ones.

I'm scared! I heard all dentists have four hands, two heads, and are *Yank*-ee fans. After your teeth are taken out, they give you toothpaste to stick 'em back in.

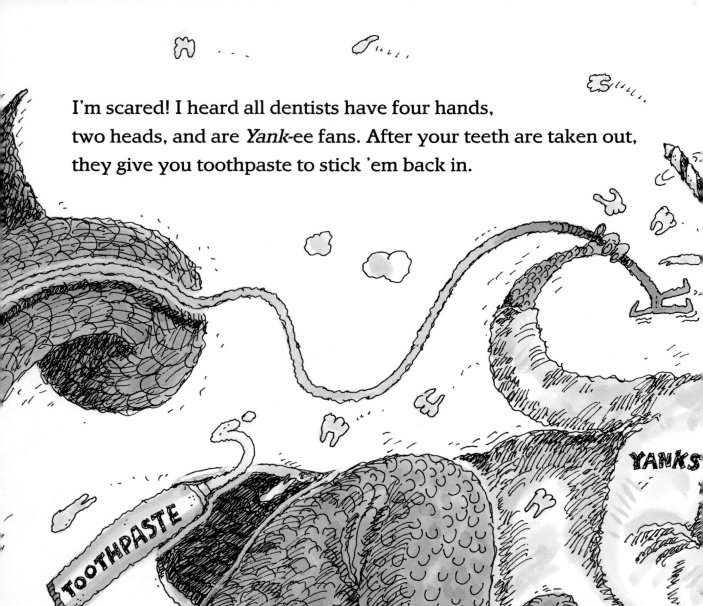

One kid said a dentist gave his cousin gas. I hope it was unleaded.

Then he drilled him.

Another kid said a dentist put *caps* on his brother's teeth.
His mouth must have looked like a Little League team.

Penny said her aunt has *crowns* on hers.

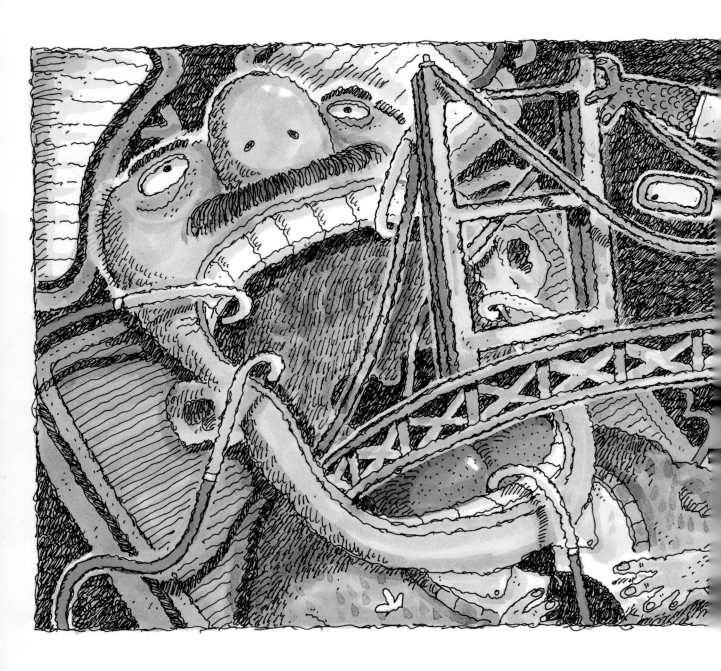

"Big deal," said Derek. "A dentist put a bridge in *my* uncle's mouth."

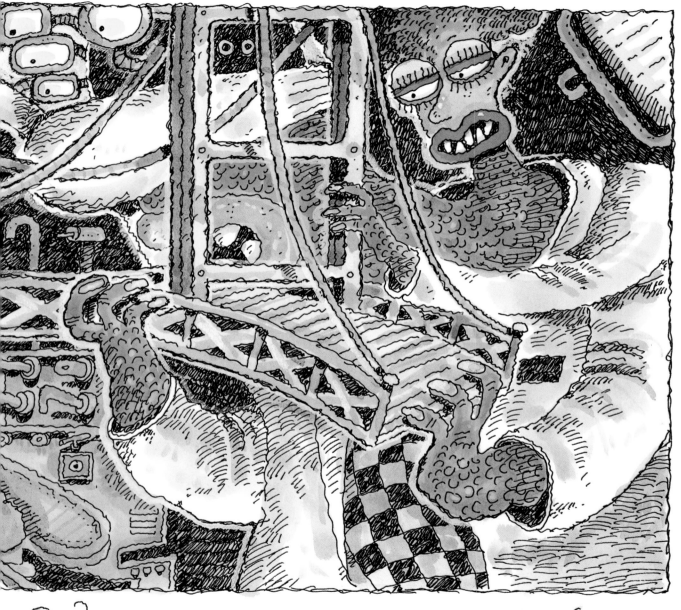

FLOSS

Wow, I hope it wasn't the Golden Gate!

NOODLE

He also said his dad has a whole root canal in his mouth—

sounds *Erie* to me.

My best friend, Eric, is going to a special dinosaur dentist called
an *ORTHODON*, who's giving him a good bite.
I told him to brace himself.

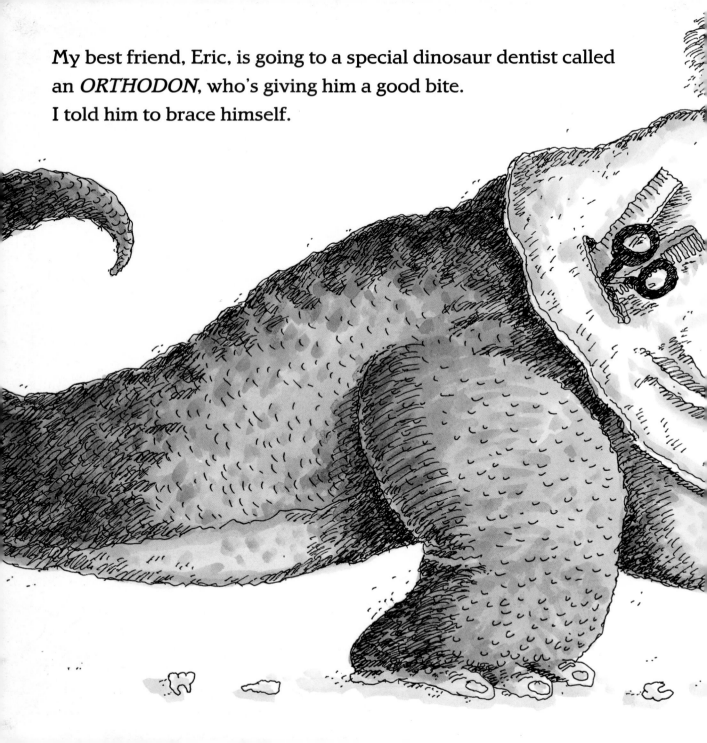

My grandpa told me my grandma's teeth are like stars—

they come out at night.

Mrs. Green says each tooth has its own name.

I thought they all had *my* name and were just called "Hubie's teeth."

Well, *my* teeth are staying in *my* mouth!

I DON'T HAVE TEETH.

Oh, no, we're on our way to the nurse's office.

EYE TOOTH

We line up by the door and go in—one by one.

I don't hear any screams *yet*. I'm polite and let everyone go ahead of me. But finally, it's *my* turn. . . .

I go in...there's a man in a mask sitting there.
And it isn't the Lone Ranger.

Dr. Payne tells me to open wide and looks in my mouth with a little mirror. Then he pats me on the head, gives me a new toothbrush, and tells me to use it every day.

← BABY TOOTH

Hey, that wasn't so bad. I got out of there with all my teeth,
a new toothbrush, and a great big smile!

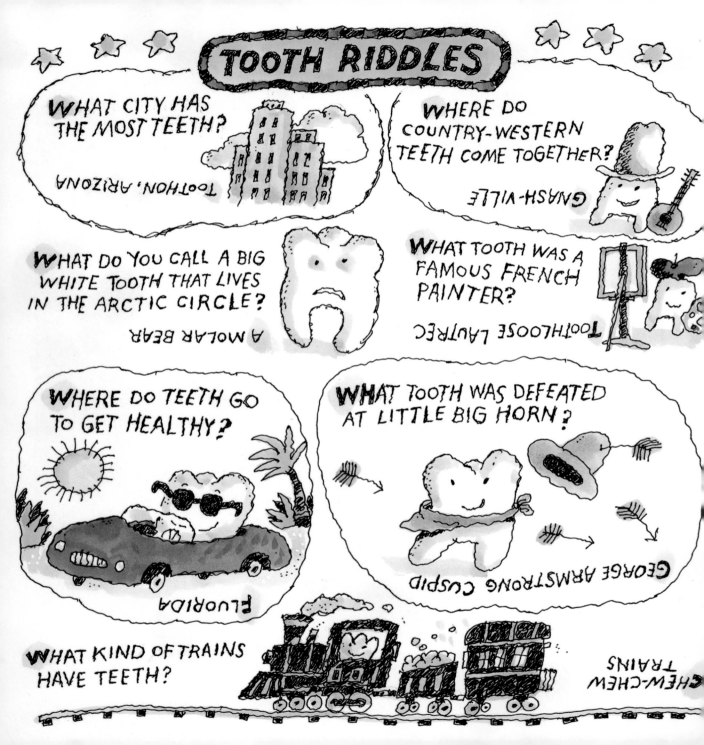